致敬译界巨匠许渊冲先生

许渊冲译
诗经·颂

BOOK OF POETRY
Book of Hymns

— 译 —

中国出版集团
中译出版社

目录
Contents

清庙之什

002　　清　庙
　　　　King Wen's Temple

002　　维天之命
　　　　King Wen Deified

004　　维　清
　　　　King Wen's Statutes

004　　烈　文
　　　　King Cheng's Inaugural Address

006　　天　作
　　　　Mount Qi

008　　昊天有成命
　　　　King Cheng's Hymn

010　　我　将
　　　　King Wu's Sacrificial Hymn

010　　时　迈
　　　　King Wu's Progress

012　　执　竞
　　　　Kings Cheng and Kang

014　　思　文
　　　　Hymn to the Lord of Corn

臣工之什

018　　臣　工
　　　　Husbandry

020　　噫　嘻
　　　　King Kang's Prayer

022	振 鹭	
	The Guest Assisting at Sacrifice	
022	丰 年	
	Thanksgiving	
024	有 瞽	
	Temple Music	
026	潜	
	Sacrifice of Fish	
026	雍	
	King Wu's Prayer to King Wen	
030	载 见	
	King Cheng's Sacrifice to King Wu	
030	有 客	
	Guests at The Sacrifice	
032	武	
	Hymn to King Wu Great and Bright	

闵予小子之什

034	闵予小子	
	Elegy on King Wu	
034	访 落	
	King Cheng's Ascension to The Throne	
036	敬 之	
	King Cheng's Consultation	
038	小 毖	
	King Cheng's Self-criticism	

040	载 芟	Cultivation of the Ground
044	良 耜	Hymn of Thanksgiving
046	丝 衣	Supplementary Sacrifice
048	酌	The Martial King
050	桓	Hymn to King Wu
050	赉	King Wu's Hymn to King Wen
052	般	The King's Progress
052	駉	Horses
056	有 駜	The Ducal Feast
058	泮 水	The Poolside Hall
066	閟 宫	Hymn to Marquis of Lu
080	那	Hymn to King Tang
082	烈 祖	Hymn to Ancestor

084　　　　玄　鸟
　　　　　　The Swallow

088　　　　长　发
　　　　　　The Rise of Shang

094　　　　殷　武
　　　　　　Hymn to King Wu Ding

颂

Book of Hymns

清庙之什

清 庙①

於②穆③清庙，	啊！深沉清静的宗庙，
肃雍显相④。	助祭公侯严肃雍容。
济济⑤多士，	众位执事威仪整齐，
秉文之德。	文王德行铭记在心。
对越⑥在天，	遥对文王在天之灵，
骏奔走在庙。	奔走在庙庭健步如飞。
不⑦显不承，	光大祖德泽被后世，
无射⑧于人斯！	人民崇敬仰慕无穷。

维⑨天之命

维天之命，	想来天道运行不悖，
於穆不已。	庄严肃穆永不停歇。
於乎不显，	多么显赫啊光明无限，
文王之德之纯！	文王的德行真纯正！

---

① 清：清明。清庙，供奉清明有德先祖的宗庙。
② 於：叹词，相当于"啊"。
③ 穆：严肃美好的样子。
④ 相：助祭的公侯。
⑤ 济济：多而整齐的样子。
⑥ 越：于。
⑦ 不：同"丕"，发语词。
⑧ 射（yì）：无射，无穷无尽。
⑨ 维：同"惟"，想的意思。

First Decade of Hymns of Zhou

King Wen's Temple[1]

Solemn's the temple still;
Princes their duties fulfil.
Numerous officers,
Virtuous King Wen's followers,
Worship his soul on high,
Whom they hurry to glorify.
There are none but revere
Tirelessly their ancestor dear.

King Wen Deified[2]

Great Heaven goes its way
Without cease and for aye.
O King Wen's virtue great
Will likewise circulate.

---

[1] This was the first hymn celebrating the reverential manner in which a sacrifice to King Wen (1184—1134 B. C.) was performed.
[2] This hymn celebrating King Wen's virtue as comparable to that of Heaven was sung when King Cheng performed a sacrifice to his grandfather in 1110 B. C.

假①以溢②我，	善道仁政令我平静，
我其收之。	我们应当好好继承。
骏惠③我文王，	遵循先祖文王的德行，
曾孙笃之。	子子孙孙都要身体力行。

维 清

维清缉熙④，	周朝政治多清明，
文王之典⑤。	文王真是能征善战。
肇禋⑥，	祭天征伐由他始，
迄用有成，	直到武王成功业，
维周之祯⑦。	这正是周朝的祥瑞。

烈 文⑧

| 烈文辟公⑨， | 文德双全的众诸侯， |
| 锡⑩兹祉福。 | 先王赐给你们大福祥。 |

① 假：通"嘉"，指仁政。
② 溢：通"谧"，静谧，平静。
③ 骏惠：顺从。
④ 缉熙：光明。
⑤ 典：当指文王用兵打仗之兵法。
⑥ 肇禋（yīn）：开始祭天。
⑦ 祯：祥瑞。
⑧ 烈文：有功与德。
⑨ 辟公：指诸侯。
⑩ 锡：通"赐"，赏赐。

His virtue overflows
And in his descendants grows.
Whatever King Wen has done
Will profit his grandson.

King Wen's Statutes[①]

The world is clear and bright;
King Wen's statutes shed light.
Begin by sacrificial rite
And end by victory great.
God, bless Zhou's State!

King Cheng's Inaugural Address[②]

O princes bright and brave
Favored by former kings!

---

① This was the third hymn appropriate at some sacrifice to King Wen and celebrating his statutes. It was sung to accompany the performance of the dance of King Wen, which consisted in going through a number of bodily movements and evolutions, intending to illustrate the style of fighting introduced by Wen in his various Wars.
② This hymn was made on the occasion of King Cheng's accession to the government in 1109 B. C. when he thus addressed the princes who had assisted him in the ancestral temple.

惠①我无②疆，	从今永远爱戴周朝，
子孙保之。	子孙永葆福无穷。
无封靡③于尔邦，	别让你国有大罪，
维王其崇④之。	我王对你才敬重。
念兹戎功，	想起你祖上的大功劳，
继序⑤其皇之。	要继承和发扬广大。
无竞⑥维人，	得到贤人最重要，
四方其训⑦之。	四方才会竞相归顺。
不显维德，	先王德行昭明，
百辟其刑之。	天下诸侯竞相模仿。
於乎！前王不忘。	啊！先王的功德铭记在心。

天 作⑧

天作高山⑨，	巍峨岐山浑然天成，
大王荒⑩之。	大王拓展疆土苦心经营。
彼作矣，	大王开创沃野千里，
文王康⑪之。	文王安抚百姓安康。

① 惠：爱。
② 无：毋。
③ 封靡：大罪过。
④ 崇：尊敬。
⑤ 继序：继承。
⑥ 无竞：不刚强，意为恭谦有礼。
⑦ 训：通"顺"。
⑧ 作：生的意思。
⑨ 高山：指岐山。
⑩ 荒：扩大治理的意思。
⑪ 康：使安乐，使安康。

Boundless blessings we have
Will pass to our offsprings.
Don't sin against your state
And you'll be honored as before.
Think of your service great
You may enlarge still more.
Try to employ wise men,
Your influence will spread from land to land.
Try to practise virtue then
Your good example will forever stand.
O of all things,
Forget not former kings!

Mount Qi[①]

Heaven made lofty hill
For former kings to till.
King Tai worked the land
For King Wen to expand.

---

① This hymn was appropriate to a sacrifice to King Tai who labored the land at the foot of Mount Qi (Poem "The Rise of Zhou").

彼徂①矣，　　　　　　　率领众民聚集岐山，
岐有夷②之行③，　　　　岐山的道路平又广，
子孙保之。　　　　　　　子孙永葆世代盛昌。

昊天有成命④

昊天有成命，　　　　　　苍天早已有命令，
二后⑤受之。　　　　　　文王武王受命为君主。
成王不敢康，　　　　　　成王不敢贪图安逸，
夙夜基命⑥宥⑦密⑧。　　日夜勤敬治国安邦。
於缉熙，　　　　　　　　文武事业更光明，
单⑨厥心，　　　　　　　忠诚之心治国，
肆⑩其靖之！　　　　　　天下一定能太平！

① 徂：到，去。
② 夷：平坦。
③ 行：道路。
④ 昊天：指苍天。成命，明确的命令。
⑤ 后：君王。二后，指文王、武王。
⑥ 基：谋。命，政令。
⑦ 宥：语气助词。
⑧ 密：勤勉。
⑨ 单：忠诚。
⑩ 肆：巩固。

The former kings are gone;
The mountain path is good to travel on.
O ye son and grandson,
Pursue what your forefathers have begun!

King Cheng's Hymn[①]

By great Heaven's decrees
Two kings with power were blessed,
King Cheng dare not live at ease
But day and night does his best
To rule the State in peace
And pacify east and west.

---

① This hymn was appropriate to a sacrifice to King Cheng (reigned 1109—1076 B. G.), son of King Wu and grandson of King Wen.

我 将[1]

我将我享[2]，	我把烹好的祭品献上，
维羊维牛，	既有牛来又有羊，
维天其右[3]之。	希望上帝保佑交好运。
仪式[4]刑[5]文王之典，	效法文王的典章制度，
日靖[6]四方。	每日谋划安定四方。
伊嘏[7]文王，	伟大圣明周文王，
既右飨之。	享受祭祀神灵来到。
我其夙夜，	我将日夜勤国政，
畏天之威，	崇敬上帝威灵遵循天道，
于时[8]保之。	保证国家的太平功造成。

时 迈[9][10]

时迈其邦，	出发巡视诸侯国，
昊天其子之，	上帝视我为子嗣，
实右[11]序[12]有周。	保佑周朝国运恒昌。

① 将：奉献。
② 享：祭献。
③ 右：佑。
④ 仪式：法度。
⑤ 刑：效法。
⑥ 靖：安定。
⑦ 嘏：伟大。
⑧ 于时：于是。
⑨ 时：语气助词。
⑩ 迈：行，指巡视、视察。
⑪ 右：同"佑"。
⑫ 序：助。

King Wu's Sacrificial Hymn[1]

I offer sacrifice
Of ram and bull so nice.
May Heaven bless my state!
I observe King Wen's statutes great;
I'll pacify the land.
O King Wen grand!
Come down and eat, I pray.
Do I not night and day
Revere Almighty Heaven?
May your favor to me be given!

King Wu's Progress[2]

A progress through the state is done.
O Heaven, bless your son!
O bless the Zhou House up and down!

---

[1] This hymn was appropriate to a sacrifice to King Wen in the hall of audience where King Wu assembled all the princes to undertake an expedition against the last king of Shang in 1121 B.C.
[2] This hymn was appropriate to King Wu's sacrifice to Heaven and to the spirits of the Mountains and Rivers on a progress through the kingdom after the overthrow of the Shang Dynasty in 1121 B.C.

薄言震之，	刚刚出兵讨伐纣王，
莫不震叠①。	天下诸侯莫不惊慌。
怀柔②百神，	祭祀四方山川神灵，
及河乔岳③。	遍及大河与高山。
允④王维后。	武王真是昭彰后世的好君王。
明昭有周，	大周德行光明照四方，
式⑤序在位。	百官都贤良忠诚。
载戢⑥干戈，	收起干戈，
载櫜⑦弓矢。	装好弓箭。
我求懿德⑧，	前去访求有德之士，
肆⑨于时夏。	遍施善政天下四方，
允王保之。	周王定能保土封疆。

执⑩ 竞⑪

执竞武王，	武王制服强暴，
无竞维烈⑫。	功业举世无双。

① 叠：通"慑"，惊惧。
② 怀柔：安抚、取悦。
③ 乔岳：高山。
④ 允：确实。
⑤ 式：发语词。
⑥ 戢：收藏。
⑦ 櫜（tuó）：盛弓矢的袋子。
⑧ 懿德：有美德的人。
⑨ 肆：实行。
⑩ 执：制服。
⑪ 竞：强暴，这里指商纣王。
⑫ 烈：功业。

Our victory is so great
That it shakes state on state.
We revere gods for ever
Of mountain and of river.
Our king is worthy of the crown.

Zhou's House is bright and full of grace:
Each lord is in his proper place,
With spears and shields stored up in rows,
And in their cases arrows and bows.
The king will do his best
To rule the kingdom east and west.
O may our king be blessed!

Kings Cheng and Kang[①]

King Wu was full of might;
He built a career bright.

---

① This hymn was appropriate to a sacrifice to Kings Wu, Cheng and Kang.

不显成康①，	全国局面安定，
上帝是皇②。	上帝对他也赞扬。
自彼成康，	由于局面安定，
奄有四方，	才一统天下拥四方，
斤斤③其明。	武王盖世英明。
钟鼓喤喤，	鸣钟擂鼓喤喤响，
磬筦④将将⑤，	击磬吹管声铿锵，
降福穰穰⑥。	上天为你多降福。
降福简简，	鸿福大无边，
威仪反反⑦。	祭礼多端庄。
既醉既饱，	神灵酒足饭饱后，
福禄来反。	再降福禄予武王。

思⑧ 文⑨

思文后稷，	先王后稷有文德，
克⑩配彼天。	功德堪比上天。
立⑪我烝民⑫，	养育我们的百姓，

① 成康：成就安定的局面。
② 皇：嘉赏。
③ 斤斤：精明的样子。
④ 筦：同"管"，一种竹制乐器。
⑤ 将将：同"锵锵"。
⑥ 穰穰：众多的样子。
⑦ 反反：慎重的样子。
⑧ 思：语气助词。
⑨ 文：文德，指建设国内的功德，与"武功"相对。
⑩ 克：能。
⑪ 立：养育。
⑫ 烝民，百姓。

God gives Cheng and Kang charge
This glory to enlarge.
Kings Cheng and Kang are blessed
To rule from east to west.
How splendid is their reign!
Hear drums' and bells' refrain.
Hear stones and flutes resound.
With blessings we are crowned.
Blessings come to our side:
Our lords look dignified.
We are drunk and well fed;
Blessings come on our head.

Hymn to the Lord of Corn[①]

O Lord of Corn so bright,
You're at God's left or right.
You gave people grain-food;

[①] This hymn was appropriate to the border sacrifice when Hou Ji, the Lord of Corn, was worshipped as the correlate of God (Poem "Hou Ji, the Lord of Corn").

莫匪尔极[1]。　　　　　　人人受您的恩惠。
贻我来牟[2],　　　　　　留给我们大麦小麦,
帝命率[3]育。　　　　　　天命养育人民。
无此疆尔界,　　　　　　农政不再分疆界,
陈常[4]于时夏。　　　　　全国上下都施行。

① 极:最,极大的恩惠。
② 来牟:小麦和大麦。
③ 率:用。
④ 常:农政。

None could do us more good.
God makes us live and eat;
You told us to plant wheat,
Not to define our border
But to live in good order.

臣工之什

臣 工①

嗟嗟②臣工，	群臣百官啊，
敬尔在公。	公事需努力。
王厘③尔成，	周王赐你耕作法，
来④咨⑤来茹⑥。	你要细致钻研。
嗟嗟保介⑦，	农官田官啊，
维⑧莫⑨之春。	暮春正要抓紧农事。
亦又何求？	你们还有啥要求？
如何新畲⑩？	生田熟田怎么种？
於⑪皇⑫来牟，	麦种壮实多肥美，
将受厥⑬明。	收成一定会很好。
明⑭昭上帝，	光明伟大的上帝，

---

① 臣工：大臣、官员。
② 嗟嗟：发语词。
③ 厘：通"赉"，赐予。
④ 来：是。
⑤ 咨：商量，询问。
⑥ 茹：忖度。
⑦ 保介：田官。
⑧ 维：是。
⑨ 莫：同"暮"。
⑩ 畲：开垦了三年的熟田。
⑪ 於：赞叹词。
⑫ 皇：美好。
⑬ 厥：其，它的。
⑭ 明：收成。

Second Decade of Hymns of Zhou

Husbandry[1]

Ah! Ye ministers dear,
Attend to duties here.
The king's set down the rule,
You Should know to the full.
Ah! Ye officers dear,
It is now late spring here.
What do you seek to do?
Tend the fields old and new.
Wheat grows lush in the field.
What an enormous yield!
Ah! Heaven bright and clear

---

[1] This was instructions given to the officers of husbandry, probably after the sacrifice in spring for a good year.

迄^①用康年。　　　　　　　请赐我们丰收年。
命我众人，　　　　　　　命令我的农夫们，
庤^②乃钱^③镈^④，　　　　　备全铁锹和锄头，
奄^⑤观铚艾^⑥。　　　　　　收割就要开始了。

噫 嘻^⑦

噫嘻成王！　　　　　　　周王向苍天祈祷呼唤，
既昭^⑧假^⑨尔。　　　　　　一片虔诚上达天帝。
率时^⑩农夫，　　　　　　　率领农夫们下地，
播厥百谷。　　　　　　　安排播种百谷。
骏^⑪发^⑫尔私^⑬，　　　　　迅速开发私田，
终三十里。　　　　　　　三十里地都种遍。
亦服^⑭尔耕，　　　　　　　大家一起来耕作，
十千维耦^⑮。　　　　　　　万人耦耕在田间。

① 迄：至。
② 庤（zhì）：准备。
③ 钱（jiǎn）：铁锹。
④ 镈：锄头。
⑤ 奄：同。
⑥ 铚艾：收割。
⑦ 噫嘻：祈祷天神的呼喊声。
⑧ 昭：表明。
⑨ 假：达，至。
⑩ 时：是，此。
⑪ 骏：迅速。
⑫ 发：开发。
⑬ 私：私田。
⑭ 服：从事。
⑮ 耦：二人并耕的耕作方法。

Will give us a good year.
Men, get ready to wield
Your sickles, spuds and hoes
And reap harvest in rows.

King Kang's Prayer[1]

O King Cheng in the sky,
Please come down from on high.
See us lead the campaign
To sow all kinds of grain,
And till our fields with glee
All over thirty li!
Ten thousand men in pairs
Plough the land with the shares.

---

[1] This hymn was said to be King Kang's prayer to King Cheng for a good year.

振① 鹭

振鹭于飞,	一群白鹭展翅飞翔,
于彼西雍②。	在西边大泽之上。
我客戾③止,	我有贵客光临,
亦有斯容④。	他也仪容高洁。
在彼无恶,	他在本国无人怨,
在此无斁⑤。	来到我邦受敬仰。
庶几夙夜,	望你日夜勤勉国事,
以永终⑥誉。	美名长存天下颂扬。

丰 年

丰年多黍多稌⑦,	丰年黍米稻谷多,
亦有高廪⑧,	粮仓高大全装满,
万亿⑨及秭⑩。	成万成亿真不少。
为酒为醴,	酿成醇酒和甜酒,

---

① 振:群飞的样子。
② 雍:水泽。
③ 戾:至。
④ 斯容:好仪容。
⑤ 无斁(yì):没有人讨厌。
⑥ 终:即"众"。
⑦ 稌:稻谷。
⑧ 廪:粮仓。
⑨ 亿:周代十万为亿。
⑩ 秭(zǐ):数量名,一万亿为一秭。

The Guest Assisting at Sacrifice[①]

Rows of egrets in flight
Over the marsh in the west.
Like those birds dressed in white,
Here comes our noble guest.
He's loved in his own State;
He is welcome in ours.
Be it early or late,
His fame for ever towers.

Thanksgiving[②]

Millet and rice abound this year;
High granaries stand far and near.
There are millions of measures fine;
We make from them spirits and wine
And offer them to ancestors dear.

[①] This hymn celebrated the representative of the former dynasty who had come to court to assist at sacrifice. It might have been sung when the king was dismissing the guest in the ancestral temple.
[②] This ode of thanksgiving for a plentiful year was used at the sacrifice in autumn and winter.

烝畀①祖妣。 进献先妣与先考。
以洽②百礼， 配合各种祭品，
降福孔皆。 普降恩泽福星照。

有 瞽③

有瞽有瞽， 盲乐师啊盲乐师，
在周之庭。 排列在周庙大庭上。
设业④设虡⑤， 钟鼓架子都摆好，
崇牙⑥树羽⑦。 架上饰有彩色羽毛。
应田县鼓⑧， 小鼓大鼓与悬鼓，
鞉⑨磬⑩柷⑪圉⑫。 鞉磬柷圉列成道。
既备乃奏， 乐器齐备就演奏，
箫管备举。 笛子排箫也备好。
喤喤厥声， 乐音和谐又洪亮，
肃雍和鸣。 徐缓肃穆好技巧。

① 畀：给予。
② 洽：配合。
③ 瞽：盲乐官。
④ 业：悬挂钟、磬的木架横梁上的锯齿状大板。
⑤ 虡（jù）：悬挂钟、磬的木架。
⑥ 崇牙：业上用来悬挂乐器的木钉。
⑦ 树羽：崇牙上装饰的五彩羽毛。
⑧ 应田县鼓：各种各样的鼓。县，通"悬"。
⑨ 鞉（táo）：摇鼓。
⑩ 磬：玉石制的古代打击乐器。
⑪ 柷：木质漆桶状的打击乐器，击柷表示音乐的开始。
⑫ 圉：古击乐器，状如伏虎，背上有二十七锯齿，以木尺划之发声，击圉表示音乐的结束。

Then we perform all kinds of rite
And call down blessings from
Heaven bright.

Temple Music[①]

Musicians blind, musicians blind,
Come to the temple court behind.
The plume-adorned posts stand
With teeth-like frames used by the band;
From them suspend drums large and small,
And sounding stones withal.
Music is played when all's complete;
We hear pan-pipe, flute and drumbeat.
What sacred melody
And solemn harmony!

---

① This hymn was made on the occasion of the Duke of Zhou's completing his instruments of music and announcing the fact in a grand performance in the temple of King Wen.

先祖是听,	先祖神灵来欣赏,
我客戾止,	我有贵宾也光临,
永观厥成。	一曲奏毕称奇妙。

潜[1]

猗与[2]漆沮[3],	漆水沮水真美啊,
潜有多鱼。	鱼儿深藏在水里。
有鳣[4]有鲔[5],	有鲤鱼也有鲟鱼,
鲦[6]鲿[7]鰋[8]鲤。	还有鲿、鲦、鲇和鲤。
以享以祀,	用来供奉祖先,
以介景福。	求降鸿福无边。

雍

有来雍雍[9],	来时雍容和睦,
至止肃肃[10]。	到此恭敬严肃。

[1] 潜:深藏。
[2] 猗与:感叹词。
[3] 漆、沮:周代的两条河。
[4] 鳣:鲤鱼。
[5] 鲔:鲟鱼。
[6] 鲦:百条鱼。
[7] 鲿:黄颊鱼。
[8] 鰋:鲇鱼。
[9] 雍雍:和睦庄重的样子。
[10] 肃肃:严肃恭敬的样子。

Dear ancestors, give ear;
Dear visitors, come here!
You will enjoy our song
And wish it to last long.

Sacrifice of Fish[1]

In Rivers Ju and Qi
Fish in warrens we see.
There're sturgeos large and small,
Mudfish, carp we enthral
For temple sacrifice
That we may be blessed twice.

King Wu's Prayer to King Wen[2]

We come in harmony;
We stop in gravity,

---

[1] This hymn was sung in the last month of winter and in spring when the king presented a fish in the ancestral temple as an act of duty and an acknowledgement that it was to his ancestors favor that the king and the people were indebted for the supplies of food which they received from the waters.

[2] This prayer was said to be appropriate at a sacrifice by King Wu to his father Wen.

相①维辟公②，	诸侯公卿助祭，
天子穆穆。	天子仪容端庄。
於荐③广牡④，	进献肥美牲畜，
相予肆祀⑤。	帮我摆好祭品。
假⑥哉皇考⑦，	伟大光荣的先王，
绥⑧予孝子。	保佑我这个孝子。
宣哲⑨维人，	百官智慧通达，
文武维后。	君王文韬武略。
燕⑩及皇天，	上天保佑周朝安宁，
克昌厥后。	子孙后代繁荣昌盛。
绥我眉寿⑪，	赐予我平安长寿，
介以繁祉⑫。	保佑我福禄无疆。
既右⑬烈考，	既请先父受祭享，
亦右文母⑭。	又请先母来品尝。

① 相：助祭。
② 辟公，诸侯。
③ 荐：献祭。
④ 广牡，肥壮的公畜。
⑤ 肆祀：陈设祭品。
⑥ 假：美、嘉。
⑦ 皇考：指文王，是武王对去世父亲的美称。
⑧ 绥：安抚。
⑨ 宣哲：聪明智慧。
⑩ 燕：安。
⑪ 眉寿：长寿。
⑫ 繁祉：多福。
⑬ 右：通"侑"，劝侑。
⑭ 文母：文王的妻子大姒。

The princes at the side
Of the king dignified.
"I present this bull nice
And set forth sacrifice
To royal father great.
Bless your filial son and his state!

"You're a sage we adore,
A king in peace and war.
O give prosperity
To Heaven and posterity!

"Bless me with a life long,
With a state rich and strong!
I pray to father I revere
And to my mother dear."

载① 见

载见辟王，	诸侯开始来朝周王，
曰求厥章②。	考求车服之类典章。
龙旗阳阳，	龙纹旗帜多么明亮，
和铃央央。	车上的铃儿响叮当。
鞗革③有鸧④，	辔头装饰金碧辉煌，
休有烈光。	华丽美好闪耀光芒。
率见昭考⑤，	率领众人祭奠武王，
以孝以享。	敬献祭品虔行祭享。
以介眉寿，	祈求赐予年寿绵长，
永言保之。	永保子孙得安康，
思皇多祜，	大福大禄又吉祥。
烈文辟公。	有功有德众位诸侯，
绥以多福，	神灵多多赐福禄，
俾缉熙于纯嘏⑥。	使我前途光明无疆。

有 客

有客有客，	远方有客来我家，
亦白其马。	驾着一匹白骏马。

---

① 载：初始。
② 章：泛指关于车、服装方面的典章制度。
③ 鞗革：马缰绳。
④ 有鸧（qiāng）：形容车马缰绳上的金饰非常艳丽。
⑤ 昭考：此处指周武王。
⑥ 嘏：福。

King Cheng's Sacrifice to King Wu[①]

The lords appear before the king
To learn the rules he ordains.
The dragon flags are bright
And the carriage bells ring.
Glitter the golden reins,
His splendor at its height.
The filial king leads the throng
Before his father's shrine.
He prays to be granted life long
And to maintain his rights divine.
May Heaven bless his state!
The princes brave and bright
Be given favors great
That they may serve at left and right.

Guests at The Sacrifice[②]

Our guests alight
From horses white.

---

① This hymn was appropriate to an occasion when the feudal princes were assisting King Cheng at a sacrifice to King Wu in 1113 B. C.
② This ode celebrated the Viscount of Wei on one of his appearances at the capital and assisting at the sacrifice in the ancestral temple of Zhou. Uncle of the last king of the Shang Dynasty, he was made Duke of Song to continue the sacrifices of the House of Shang.

有萋有且①,　　　　　　　　随从人员一大群,
敦琢其旅。　　　　　　　　每位都品德良好。

有客宿宿,　　　　　　　　客人头夜在此宿,
有客信信②。　　　　　　　三天四天一再留。
言授之絷,　　　　　　　　最好拿条绊马绳,
以絷其马。　　　　　　　　拴住马脚不让行。

薄言追③之,　　　　　　　客人将去我饯行,
左右绥之。　　　　　　　　文武百官同相送。
既有淫威,　　　　　　　　客人既已受款待,
降福孔夷。　　　　　　　　请神赐予更大福。

武

於皇武王!　　　　　　　　多么伟大的周武王啊!
无竞维烈。　　　　　　　　丰功伟业举世无双。
允文文王,　　　　　　　　文德显著周文王,
克开厥后。　　　　　　　　万代的基业他开创。
嗣武受之,　　　　　　　　武王继成受天命,
胜殷遏刘④,　　　　　　　制止杀戮胜殷商,
耆⑤定尔功。　　　　　　　巩固政权绩辉煌。

① 萋、且:随从众多的样子。
② 信:住两夜。一宿为宿,再宿为信。
③ 追:饯行,送别。
④ 刘:杀,征伐。
⑤ 耆(zhǐ):致使;达到。

Their train is long,
A noble throng.

Stay here one night;
Fasten their horses tight.
Stay here three nights or four;
Let no horse leave the door!

Escort guests on their way;
Say left and right, "Good day!"
Say "Good day" left and right
Till day turns into night.

Hymn to King Wu Great and Bright[①]

O King Wu great and bright,
Matchless in main and might.
King Wen beyond compare
Opened the way for his heir.
King Wu after his sire
Quelled Yin's tyrannic fire.
His fadme grows higher and higher.

---

① This hymn was sung in the ancestral temple to the music regulating the dance in honor of the achievements of King Wu.

闵予小子之什

闵[1] 予小子

闵予小子，	可怜我年纪轻轻，
遭家不造[2]，	家门遭难真不幸，
嬛嬛[3]在疚[4]。	孤苦无依整日哀叹。
於乎皇考！	称赞伟大先父周武王！
永世克孝。	终生能把孝道行。
念兹皇祖，	追念我的祖父周文王，
陟降[5]庭止。	任用臣子公正无私。
维予小子，	想我嗣位年纪轻，
夙夜敬止。	早晚办事应恭敬。
於乎皇王！	文王武王请放心！
继序[6]思不忘。	继承大业永铭记。

访[7] 落

访予落止，	执政之初认真谋划，
率[8]时昭考。	要遵循武王行德政。

[1] 闵：通"悯"，怜悯。
[2] 不造：不幸，不详。
[3] 嬛嬛：孤独无依。
[4] 疚：忧伤，痛苦。
[5] 陟降：上下，即提升或降级的意思。
[6] 序：绪，事业。
[7] 访：谋划，商讨。
[8] 率：遵循。

Third Decade of Hymns of Zhou

Elegy on King Wu[①]

Alas! How sad am I!
Over my deceased father I cry.
Lonely, I'm in distress
To lose my father whom gods bless.
Filial all your life long,
You loved grandfather strong
As if he were ever in courtyard.
Fatherless, I am thinking hard
Of you both night and day.
O kings to be remembered for aye!

King Cheng's Ascension to The Throne[②]

I take counsel on early days:
How to follow my father's ways?

---

① This elegy was appropriate to the young King Cheng, declaring his sentiments in the temple of his father.
② This seemed to be a sequel to the former hymn. The young king told of his difficulties and incompetences, asked for counsel to help to follow the example of his father, stated how he meaned to do so and concluded with an appeal to King Wu.

於乎悠哉!	任务重大道路远啊!
朕未有艾①。	少有经验无甚才。
将予就之②,	帮我实行先王的章法,
继犹判涣③。	继续谋求大业成。
维予小子,	想我如今年纪轻,
未堪家多难。	家国多难担承不起。
绍④庭上下,	先父遵循先人法度,
陟降厥家。	用人得当国家安宁。
休⑤矣皇考,	武王神灵真英明,
以保明⑥其身。	保佑我身得安宁。

敬⑦ 之

敬之敬之!	为人处世要小心谨慎!
天维显思。	天理昭昭最明显。
命不易哉!	保持国运真困难!
无曰高高在上。	莫说苍天高高在上。
陟降厥士⑧,	任用群臣要顺应天意,
日监在兹。	每日监视这下边。
维予小子,	想我年轻人刚刚即位,

① 艾:阅历。
② 将予就之:指将遵循先人的法典。
③ 判涣:分散,使广大。
④ 绍:继承。
⑤ 休:美。
⑥ 明:勉励。
⑦ 敬:警戒。
⑧ 士:通"事"。

Ah! But he is far above me
And to reach him I am not free.
Please help me to get to his side,
To learn on what I should decide.
I am a young king not so great
To shoulder hard tasks of the state.
I will follow him up and down,
Take counsel to secure the crown.
Rest in peace, royal father dear,
O help me to be bright and clear!

King Cheng's Consultation[①]

"Be reverent, be reverent!
The Heaven's way is evident.
Do not let its favor pass by
Nor say Heaven's remote on high.
It rules over our rise and fall
And daily watches over all."
"I am a young king of our state,

[①] This dialogue might be a portion of the consultation which took place in the temple between King Cheng and his ministers. The first half was the admonition of the ministers and the second the reply of the king.

不聪①敬止。　　　　　　　　敢不听从不恭敬。
日就②月将③，　　　　　　　日积月累时常学习，
学有缉熙于光明。　　　　　　学问积渐向光明。
佛④时⑤仔肩⑥，　　　　　　群臣辅我担大任，
示我显德行。　　　　　　　　告诉我治国的美德。

小 毖⑦

予其惩⑧，　　　　　　　　　我要惩前毖后，
而毖后患。　　　　　　　　　却无人给我指引。
莫予荓蜂⑨，　　　　　　　　无人扯我去往哪里，
自求辛螫⑩。　　　　　　　　真是自寻苦辛劳。
肇允彼桃虫⑪，　　　　　　　开始以为小鹪鹩，
拚⑫飞维鸟。　　　　　　　　忽成大鸟飞上天。
未堪家多难，　　　　　　　　家国多难受不了，
予又集于蓼⑬。　　　　　　　陷入困境更难堪。

① 聪：听。
② 就：久。
③ 将：长。
④ 佛：通"弼"，辅助。
⑤ 时：是。
⑥ 仔肩，责任。
⑦ 毖：谨慎。
⑧ 惩：警戒。成语"惩前毖后"即源于此。
⑨ 荓（píng）蜂：牵引扶住的意思。
⑩ 螫（shì）：勤劳。
⑪ 桃虫：一种极小的鸟。
⑫ 拚（fān）：通"翻"，翻飞。
⑬ 蓼：水草名，其味苦辣。

But I will show reverence great.
As sun and moon shine day and night,
I will learn to be fair and bright.
Assist me to fulfill my duty
And show me high virtue and beauty!"

King Cheng's Self-criticism[①]

I blame myself for woes gone by
And guard against those of future nigh.
A wasp is a dangerous thing.
Why should I seek its painful sting?
At first only a wren is heard;
When it takes wing, it becomes a bird.
Unequal to hard tasks of the state,
I am again in a narrow strait.

---

① King Cheng acknowledged that he had erred and stated his purpose to be careful in the future; he would guard against the slightest beginning of evil and was penetrated with a sense of his own incompetencies. This piece might be considered as the conclusion of the service in the ancestral temple with which it and the previous three were connected.

载 芟①

载芟载柞②，	开始除草又除杂树，
其耕泽泽③。	接着用力耕田松土。
千耦④其耘⑤，	成千上万的农夫锄草，
徂隰⑥徂畛⑦。	走向田地的小路。
侯⑧主⑨侯伯⑩，	田主带着长子，
侯亚⑪侯旅⑫，	跟着许多子孙晚辈，
侯强⑬侯以⑭。	壮汉雇工一起劳作。
有嗿⑮其馌⑯，	送饭的人说说笑笑，
思⑰媚⑱其妇，	妇女个个样貌美好，
有依⑲其士⑳。	男子个个干劲旺盛。

① 芟（shān）：锄草。
② 柞：砍伐树木。
③ 泽泽（shì shì）：土松散的样子。
④ 耦：二人并耕。
⑤ 耘：去田间的草。
⑥ 隰：低湿的田地，即指田地所在。
⑦ 畛（zhěn）：田边的小路。
⑧ 侯：语气助词。
⑨ 主：家长。
⑩ 伯：长子。
⑪ 亚：长子以次的诸子。
⑫ 旅：众，指晚辈。
⑬ 强：指强壮有力的人。
⑭ 以：用或干。
⑮ 嗿（tǎn）：众饮食的声音。
⑯ 馌（yè）：送到田间的饭。
⑰ 思：语气助词。
⑱ 媚：美好。
⑲ 依：通"殷"，壮盛的样子。
⑳ 士：指在田中耕作的男子。

Cultivation of the Ground[1]

The grass and bushes cleared away,
The ground is ploughed at break of day.
A thousand pairs weed, hoe in hand;
They toil in old or new-tilled land.
The master comes with all his sons,
The older and the younger ones.
They are all strong and stout;
At noon they take meals out.
They love their women fair
Who take of them good care.

[1] This piece was an accompaniment of some royal sacrifice.

有略①其耜②,　　　　　　　犁锹雪亮锋利,
俶载南亩。　　　　　　　　开始耕种南面的土地。
播厥百谷,　　　　　　　　各种禾谷播种下去,
实函③斯活④。　　　　　　粒粒种子饱含生气。
驿驿其达,　　　　　　　　苗儿不断冒出来,
有厌⑤其杰⑥,　　　　　　杰出的苗儿特美,
厌厌其苗,　　　　　　　　一般地整整齐齐,
绵绵⑦其麃⑧。　　　　　　稻穗连绵颗粒饱满。
载获济济,　　　　　　　　开始收获硕果累累,
有实⑨其积⑩,　　　　　　场上粮食堆积如山,
万亿及秭⑪。　　　　　　　算来有千亿万亿。
为酒为醴⑫,　　　　　　　用来酿造醇和美酒,
烝⑬畀祖妣,　　　　　　　将它们进献给先祖,
以洽⑭百礼⑮。　　　　　　供应各种祭礼。
有飶⑯其香,　　　　　　　祭筵酒气芬芳,
邦家之光。　　　　　　　　邦国光大家庭昌盛。

① 略:锋利。
② 耜:农具名,犁头,用来插地起土。
③ 函:含藏。
④ 活:有生气的样子。
⑤ 厌:美好的样子。
⑥ 杰:先长出的苗。
⑦ 绵绵:连绵不断的样子。
⑧ 麃:禾苗的末梢。
⑨ 实:满。
⑩ 积:在露天堆积粮谷。
⑪ 秭:万亿。
⑫ 醴:甜酒。
⑬ 烝:进。
⑭ 洽:合。
⑮ 百礼,各种祭礼。
⑯ 飶(bì):本字为"苾",芬芳。

With the sharp plough they wield,
They break the southern field.
All kinds of grain they sow
Burst into life and grow,
Young shoots without end rise;
The longest strike the eyes.
The grain grows lush here and there;
The toilers weed with care.
The reapers come around;
The grain's piled up aground.
There're millions of stacks fine
To be made food or wine
For our ancestors' shrine
And for the rites divine.
The delicious food
Is glory of kinghood.

有椒其馨, 醇和的甜酒真芬芳,
胡考①之宁。 老人长寿享安康。
匪且②有且, 如此繁荣超过期望,
匪今斯今, 丰收并非破天荒,
振③古如兹。 自古就有这般景象。

良 耜

畟畟④良耜, 犁头雪亮又锋利,
俶载南亩。 先耕南边田地。
播厥百谷, 播下多种禾谷,
实函斯活。 颗颗饱含生气。
或来瞻女, 有人前来看望,
载筐及筥⑤, 拿着方箦圆筐,
其饟⑥伊黍。 送来米饭热气腾。
其笠伊纠, 头戴编织的斗笠,
其镈⑦斯赵, 挥动锄头齐心协力,
以薅⑧荼蓼⑨。 薅除杂草清理田亩。

① 考:寿考。
② 且:此,指丰收。
③ 振:起。
④ 畟畟(cè cè):形容器物锋利。
⑤ 筥(jǔ):圆形的竹筐。
⑥ 饟:"饷"的异体字,将食物给人叫作"饷"。
⑦ 镈:农具名,锄头,用来除草。
⑧ 薅:拔除田草。
⑨ 荼、蓼:两种野草。

The fragrant wine, behold!
Gives comfort to the old.
We reap not only here
But always in good cheer.
We reap not only for today
But always in our fathers' way.

Hymn of Thanksgiving[①]

Sharp are plough-shares we wield;
We plough the southern field.
All kinds of grain we sow
Burst into life and grow.
Our wives come to the ground
With baskets square and round
Of millet and steamed bread,
With straw-hat on the head.
We weed with hoe in hand
On the dry and wet land.

---

① This hymn was made for the thanksgiving to the spirits of the land and the grain in autumn and it was proper therefore that it should set forth the beginning and the end of the labors of husbandry.

茶蓼朽止，　　　　　　　　　杂草烂掉在田地，
黍稷茂止。　　　　　　　　　庄稼长得真茂盛。
获之挃挃①，　　　　　　　　挥动镰刀唰唰响，
积之栗栗②。　　　　　　　　场上粮食高堆积。
其崇如墉，　　　　　　　　　堆得城墙一般高，

其比③如栉④，　　　　　　　堆得梳篦一般密，
以开百室⑤。　　　　　　　　成千上百仓开启。
百室盈止，　　　　　　　　　仓屋全部都装满，
妇子宁止。　　　　　　　　　妇女儿童得休息。

杀时犉⑥牡，　　　　　　　　宰牛献到祭坛，
有捄⑦其角。　　　　　　　　牛角向上弯弯。
以似以续，　　　　　　　　　祭祀社稷之神，
续古之人。　　　　　　　　　永远继承先人传统。

丝 衣

丝衣其紑⑧，　　　　　　　　身着丝衣洁净鲜明，
载弁俅俅。　　　　　　　　　头戴皮帽美丽端正。

---

① 挃挃：割取禾穗的声音。
② 栗栗：众多的样子。
③ 比：排列迫近。
④ 栉：理发用具，梳篦总名。
⑤ 百室：指储藏谷子的仓屋。
⑥ 犉（rún）：牛长七尺。
⑦ 捄（qiú）：通作"觓"，角上曲而长之貌，形容匕柄的形状。
⑧ 紑（fóu）：洁净新鲜的样子。

When weeds fall in decay,
Luxuriant millets sway.
When millets rustling fall,
We reap and pile them up all
High and thick as a wall.

Like comb teeth stacks are close;
Stores are opened in rows.
Wives and children repose
When all the stores are full.

We kill a tawny bull,
Whose horns crooked appear.
We follow fathers dear
To perform rites with cheer.

Supplementary Sacrifice[①]

In silken robes clean and bright,
In temple caps for the rite,

[①] This piece belonged to the entertainment of the personator of the dead in connection with the supplementary sacrifice on the day after one of the great sacrifices in the ancestral temple.

自堂徂基①,　　　　　　　从庙堂一直到门槛,
自羊徂牛,　　　　　　　有着牛羊等做牺牲,
鼐②鼎及鼒③。　　　　　还有大鼎和小鼎。
兕觥其觩,　　　　　　　兕角杯儿弯弯如月,
旨酒思柔。　　　　　　　斟满美酒温柔清醇。
不吴④不敖,　　　　　　不敢喧哗不傲慢,
胡考之休!　　　　　　　保佑我们都长寿。

酌

於⑤铄⑥王师,　　　　　武王军队战绩辉煌,
遵养时晦⑦。　　　　　　挥兵攻取昏庸的纣王。
时纯熙⑧矣,　　　　　　一时间普天都得光明,
是用大介。　　　　　　　天降恩泽大吉祥。
我龙受之,　　　　　　　顺应天意得天下,
蹻蹻⑨王之造。　　　　　武王功业四海扬。
载用有嗣,　　　　　　　后世子孙要铭记,
实维尔公⑩允师。　　　　先人是我们好榜样。

① 基:"畿"的假借词,门槛。
② 鼐(nài):大鼎。
③ 鼒(zī):小鼎。
④ 吴:大声喧哗。
⑤ 於:赞美词。
⑥ 铄:辉煌的样子。
⑦ 时晦:不利之时。
⑧ 纯熙:明亮。
⑨ 蹻蹻:勇武的样子。
⑩ 尔公:你的先人。

The officers come from the hall
To inspect tripods large and small,
To see the sheep and oxen down and up
And rhino horns used as cup,
To see if mild is wine,
If there is noise before the shrine
In sacrifice to lords divine.

The Martial King[①]

The royal army brave and bright
Was led by King Wu in dark days
To overthrow Shang and bring back light
And establish the Zhou House's sway.
Favored by Heaven, I
Succeed the Martial King.
I'll follow him as nigh
As summer follows spring.

① This was King Cheng's hymn in praise of King Wu or the Martial King who reigned 1121—1115 B. C. It was made to announce in the temple of King Wu the completion of the dance intended to represent the achievements of the king in the overthrow of the Shang and the establishment of the Zhou dynasty. Poem "Hymn to King Wu" and the three that followed this were also sung in connection with that dance.

桓

绥①万邦,	武王平定天下万邦,
娄丰年。	年年喜获好收成。
天命匪解②。	天命在周要长久。
桓桓③武王,	武王英明又威武,
保有厥土。	拥有辽阔的疆域。
于以四方,	于是镇抚四方国,
克定厥家。	齐家治国平天下。
於昭于天,	武王光辉照天上,
皇④以间⑤之!	代替殷商享天下!

赉

文王既勤止,	文王一生太勤劳,
我应受之。	我当好好来继承。
敷⑥时绎⑦思,	施行政令要三思,
我徂⑧维求定。	天下安定是我求。
时周之命。	周王命令须奉行,
於⑨绎思!	文王政令要谨记!

① 绥:安定。
② 解:懈怠。
③ 桓桓:威武的样子。
④ 皇:君王。
⑤ 间:代。
⑥ 敷:颁布。
⑦ 绎:寻绎、不断的意思。
⑧ 徂:往。
⑨ 於:叹词。

Hymn to King Wu[1]

All the states pacified,
Heaven favors Zhou far and wide,
Rich harvest from year to year.
How mighty did King Wu appear
With his warriors and cavaliers
Guarding his four frontiers
And securing his state!
Favored by Heaven great,
Zhou replaced Shang by fate.

King Wu's Hymn to King Wen[2]

King Wen's career is done;
I will follow him as son,
Thinking of him without cease.
We have conquered Shang to seek peace.
O our royal decree
Should be done in high glee.

---

[1] This hymn was considered as a portion of the larger piece sung to the dance celebrating the merit and success of King Wu.
[2] This hymn celebrating the praise of King Wen was said to be the third of the pieces sung to the dance mentioned in the note on Poem "The Martial King".

般

於皇时周,	啊,大周的天下多壮丽,
陟其高山。	登至那座高山向下望。
嶞①山乔岳②,	小山大山都在眼前,
允犹翕③河。	合祭黄河献上美酒。
敷天之下,	普天之下的神灵,
裒④时之对,	同聚一起齐享受,
时周之命。	保佑大周国运永昌。

駉

駉駉⑤牡马,	群马雄健又高大,
在坰⑥之野。	放牧远郊和水边。
薄言駉者:	要问良马有几种:
有驈⑦有皇,	白胯黑马浅黄马。
有骊有黄,	骊马纯黑赤马黄,
以车彭彭⑧。	驾起车来强有力。
思无疆,	鲁公深谋又远虑,
思马斯臧。	马儿优良再无加。

① 嶞(duò):狭长的小山。
② 乔岳:高大的山。
③ 翕(xī):合,指合祭。
④ 裒(póu):聚集。
⑤ 駉駉(jiōng jiōng):马肥壮的样子。
⑥ 坰(jiōng):远。
⑦ 驈(yù):黑色的马白色的胯。
⑧ 彭彭(bāng bāng):马强壮有力的样子。

The King's Progress[1]

O great is the Zhou State!
I climb up mountains high
To see hills undulate
And two rivers flow by.
Gods are worshipped, I see,
Under the boundless sky,
All by royal decree.

Horses[2]

How sleek and large the horses are
Upon the plain of borders far!
What color are these horses bright?
Some black and white, some yellow light,
Some are pure black, others are bay.
What splendid chariot steeds are they!
The Duke of Lu has clear fore-sight:
He has prepared his steeds to fight.

---

[1] This hymn was said to be the fourth of the six pieces sung to the dance celebrating the greatness of Zhou and its firm possession of the kingdom, as seen in King Wu's progress.

[2] This was an ode celebrating Duke Xi of Lu (658—626 B. C.) for his constant and admirable thoughtfulness, especially as seen in the number and quality of his horses.

驷驷牡马，　　　　　　　群马高大又强壮，
在坰之野。　　　　　　　牧放远郊和水边。
薄言驷者：　　　　　　　要问良马有几种：
有骓① 有駓②，　　　　　杂色白马黄白马，
有骍有骐，　　　　　　　骍马青黑赤黄骐，
以车伓伓③。　　　　　　驾起车来有力气。
思无期，　　　　　　　　鲁公深谋又远虑，
思马斯才。　　　　　　　马儿成才真堪嘉。

驷驷牡马，　　　　　　　群马雄壮又高大，
在坰之野。　　　　　　　放在远郊近山坡。
薄言驷者：　　　　　　　要问良马有几种：
有骓④ 有骆，　　　　　　骓马青黑骆马白，
有骝有雒，　　　　　　　赤色骝马黑色雒，
以车绎绎⑤。　　　　　　驾起车来快如梭。
思无斁⑥，　　　　　　　鲁公深谋又远虑，
思马斯作。　　　　　　　马儿振作撒欢跳。

驷驷牡马，　　　　　　　群马肥壮强有劲，
在坰之野。　　　　　　　放牧郊野近山边。
薄言驷者：　　　　　　　要问良马有几种：

① 骓（zhuī）：苍白杂毛的马。
② 駓（pī）：黄白杂毛的马。
③ 伓伓（pī pī）：有力的样子。
④ 骓（tuó）：青黑色而有白鳞花纹的马。
⑤ 绎绎（yì yì）：跑得快的样子。
⑥ 斁（yì）：厌倦。

How sleek and large the horses are
Upon the plain of borders far!
What color are these horses bright?
Some piebald, others green and white;
Some brownish red, others dapple grey.
What fiery chariot steeds are they!
The Duke of Lu has good fore-sight:
He will employ his steeds in fight.

How sleek and large the horses are
Upon the plain of borders far!
What color are these steeds well trained?
Some flecked, some white and blackmaned,
Some black and white-maned, others red.
They are chariot horses well-bred.
The Duke of Lu has fine fore-sight:
He has bred and trained his steeds to fight.

How sleek and large the horses are
Upon the plain of borders far!
What color are these horses bright?

有骃①有騢②,　　　　　　　红白騢马灰白骃,
有驔③有鱼④,　　　　　　　黄脊驔马白眶驹,
以车祛祛⑤。　　　　　　　驾起车来脚步轻。
思无邪,　　　　　　　　　鲁公深谋又远虑,
思马斯徂。　　　　　　　　马儿俊美能疾行。

有 駜⑥

有駜有駜,　　　　　　　　马儿肥壮又高大,
駜彼乘黄。　　　　　　　　驾上四匹黄骠马。
夙夜在公,　　　　　　　　早晚忙碌为国家,
在公明明⑦。　　　　　　　鞠躬尽瘁无闲暇。
振振⑧鹭,　　　　　　　　一群白鹭飞上天,
鹭于下。　　　　　　　　　忽而上升忽而下。
鼓咽咽⑨,　　　　　　　　鼓儿咚咚不停响,
醉言舞,　　　　　　　　　酒醉起舞影婆娑,
于胥乐兮。　　　　　　　　大家欢乐笑开颜。

有駜有駜,　　　　　　　　马儿高大多肥壮,
駜彼乘牡。　　　　　　　　四匹公马气昂昂。

① 骃（yīn）：浅黑和白色相杂的马。
② 騢（xiá）：赤白杂毛的马。
③ 驔（diàn）：黑色黄脊的马。
④ 鱼：两眼眶有白圈的马。
⑤ 祛祛（qū qū）：强健。
⑥ 駜：马肥壮有力的样子。
⑦ 明明：操劳勤勉。
⑧ 振振：鸟群飞的声音。
⑨ 咽咽：有节奏的鼓声。

Some cream-like, others red and white;
Some white-legged, others fishlike eyed.
They drive war chariots side by side.
The Duke of Lu has grand fore-sight:
He will drive his brave steeds to fight.

The Ducal Feast[①]

Sleek and strong, sleek and strong,
Four brown steeds come along.
The officers are wise,
Stay late but early rise.
Like egrets white
Dancers alight.
The drums resound;
Tipsy, they dance aground
In happiness they are drowned.

Sleek and strong, sleek and strong,
Four stallions come along.

---

① This piece related how Duke Xi of Lu feasted together with his officers and how the officers expressed their good wishes.

夙夜在公，　　　　　　　早晚忙碌在公堂，
在公饮酒。　　　　　　　公事之余把酒尝。
振振鹭，　　　　　　　　一群白鹭飞上天，
鹭于飞。　　　　　　　　渐展羽翅高高飞。
鼓咽咽，　　　　　　　　鼓儿敲起咚咚响，
醉言归。　　　　　　　　酒醉饭饱人散场。
于胥乐兮。　　　　　　　大家心里喜洋洋。

有驰有驰，　　　　　　　马儿强壮多有劲，
驰彼乘骃①。　　　　　　四匹青马真雄壮。
夙夜在公，　　　　　　　早晚办事在公堂，
在公载燕。　　　　　　　公事之余齐举觞。
自今以始，　　　　　　　打从今年开始，
岁其有。　　　　　　　　年年都是丰收年。
君子有穀②，　　　　　　君子有德做善事，
诒孙子。　　　　　　　　子孙后代永相传。
于胥乐兮。　　　　　　　大家欢喜笑开颜。

泮　水③

思乐泮水，　　　　　　　泮水之滨喜洋洋，
薄采其芹④。　　　　　　人在水中采水芹。

---

① 骃：青黑马。
② 穀：善，福禄。
③ 泮水：水名。
④ 芹：水芹菜。

The officers drink wine;
Early and late they are fine.
Like egrets white
Dancers in flight.
The drums resound;
Drunk, they go round;
In happiness they are drowned.

Sleek and strong, sleek and strong,
Four grey steeds come along.
The officers eat food
Early and late they are good.
From now and here,
Abundant be each year!
The duke has well done,
So will his son and grandson,
They will be happy everyone.

The Poolside Hall[①]

Pleasant is the pool half-round
Where plants of cress abound.

---

① This was an ode in praise of Marquis or Duke Xi of Lu, celebrating his interest in the state college built by the poolside and his exaggerated triumph over the tribes of the Huai, celebrated in the poolside hall.

鲁侯戾止①,　　　　　　　　鲁侯大驾将光临,
言观其旂。　　　　　　　　只见大旗龙纹影。
其旂茷茷②,　　　　　　　　车上旌旗随风展,
鸾声哕哕。　　　　　　　　铃儿叮当响不停。
无小无大,　　　　　　　　百官无论大与小,
从公于③迈。　　　　　　　跟随鲁侯向前行。

思乐泮水,　　　　　　　　游乐泮水乐陶陶,
薄采其藻。　　　　　　　　人在水中采水草。
鲁侯戾止,　　　　　　　　鲁侯大驾已来到,
其马蹻蹻④。　　　　　　　马儿强健四蹄骄。
其马蹻蹻,　　　　　　　　马儿强健四蹄骄,
其音昭昭⑤。　　　　　　　随行人儿多热闹。
载色⑥载笑,　　　　　　　鲁侯和颜又悦色,
匪怒伊教。　　　　　　　　从不发怒耐心教。

思乐泮水,　　　　　　　　游乐泮水乐悠悠,
薄采其茆⑦。　　　　　　　采摘莼菜忙不休。
鲁侯戾止,　　　　　　　　鲁侯大驾已来到,
在泮饮酒。　　　　　　　　泮水岸边摆美酒。
既饮旨酒,　　　　　　　　美酒已经举杯饮,

① 戾止：到达。
② 茷茷（pèi pèi）：旗帜飘扬的样子。
③ 于：往，迈，行。
④ 蹻蹻：马强壮的样子。
⑤ 昭昭：响亮。
⑥ 色：和颜悦色。
⑦ 茆：江南的莼菜。

The Marquis of Lu comes nigh;
His dragon banners fly,
His flags wave on the wing
And his carriage bells ring.
Officers old and young
Follow him all along.

Pleasant is the pool half-round
Where water-weeds abound.
The Marquis of Lu comes near;
His horses grand appear.
His horses appear strong;
His carriage bells ring long.
With smiles and with looks bland,
He will instruct and command.

Pleasant is the pool half-round
Where mallow plants abound.
The Marquis pays a call
And drinks wine in the hall.
After wine, it is foretold,

永锡难老①。	祝君长寿年岁久。
顺彼长道②,	顺着大道向前走,
屈此群丑。	政府叛贼不用愁。
穆穆鲁侯,	鲁公端庄又威严,
敬明其德。	恭敬勤勉振朝纲。
敬慎威仪,	注意威仪有礼貌,
维民之则。	真是人民好榜样。
允文允武,	又能文来又能武,
昭假③烈祖。	英明能及诸先王。
靡有不孝,	遵循祖训无不孝,
自求伊祜。	自求福佑保吉祥。
明明鲁侯,	鲁公勤勉又努力,
克明其德。	能修品德讲法度。
既作泮宫,	已把泮宫建设好,
淮夷攸服。	淮夷人民都归顺。
矫矫④虎臣,	将帅英勇如猛虎,
在泮献馘⑤。	献敌左耳泮水旁。
淑问⑥如皋陶,	审讯得法似皋陶,
在泮献囚。	泮宫献上阶下囚。

① 老:长寿的意思。
② 长道:远路。
③ 昭假:诚心祭告。
④ 矫矫:勇武的样子。
⑤ 馘(guó):割下敌人的左耳以记功。
⑥ 淑问:善于审问。

"You will never grow old.
If along the way you go,
You will overcome the foe."

The Marquis' virtue high
Is well-known far and nigh.
His manner dignified,
He is ever people's guide.
He is bright as well as brave,
Worthy son of ancestors grave.
He is full of filial love
And seeks blessings from above.

The Marquis of Lu bright
Sheds his virtuous light.
He has built the poolside hall;
Huai tribes pay him homage all.
His tiger-like compeers
Presents the foe's left ears.
His judges wisdom show;
They bring the captive foe.

济济多士，　　　　　　百官济济人才多，
克广德心。　　　　　　鲁侯善心得传扬。
桓桓①于征，　　　　　三军威武去出征，
狄彼东南。　　　　　　平定东南去祸殃。
烝烝皇皇②，　　　　　声势盛大军容壮，
不吴不扬。　　　　　　肃静无哗列队过。
不告于讻③，　　　　　宽待俘虏不穷究，
在泮献功。　　　　　　泮宫献功赐玉帛。

角弓其觩④，　　　　　角弓弯弯硬又强，
束矢其搜。　　　　　　众箭齐发嗖嗖响。
戎车孔博⑤，　　　　　战车坚固千百辆，
徒御无斁。　　　　　　战士英勇斗志昂。
既克淮夷，　　　　　　淮夷已经被征服，
孔淑不逆。　　　　　　俯首听命不违抗。
式固尔犹⑥，　　　　　坚决执行好计谋，
淮夷卒获。　　　　　　淮夷终于得扫荡。

翩彼飞鸮⑦，　　　　　翩翩飞翔猫头鹰，
集于泮林。　　　　　　落在泮水岸边林。
食我桑黮⑧，　　　　　吃了我的紫桑葚，

① 桓桓：威武的样子。
② 烝烝皇皇：形容一种盛况。
③ 讻（xiōng）：争辩。
④ 觩：弓弯曲强硬的样子。
⑤ 博：多。
⑥ 犹：通"猷"，计谋。
⑦ 鸮：猫头鹰。
⑧ 黮（shèn）：通"葚"，桑葚。

His officers aligned
With their forces combined
Drove in martial array
Southeastern tribes away.
They came on backward way
Without noise or display.
At poolside hall they show
What they have done with the foe.

They notch their arrows long
On bows with bone made strong.
Their chariots show no fears,
With tireless charioteers.
The tribes of Huai they quell
Dare no longer rebel.
As the Marquis would have it,
The tribes, of Huai Submit.

The owls flying at ease
Settle on poolslde trees.
They eat our mulberries

怀我好音。	为我歌唱有佳音。
憬①彼淮夷,	如今淮夷有觉悟,
来献其琛。	献来珍宝表中心。
元龟象齿,	既有大龟和象牙,
大赂②南金。	还有南方珍贵金。

閟 宫③

閟宫有侐④,	姜嫄之庙多静寂,
实实⑤枚枚。	又高又大人迹稀。
赫赫姜嫄,	姜嫄光明又伟大,
其德不回⑥。	品德端正无邪瑕。
上帝是依⑦,	上帝凭依在她身,
无灾无害。	无灾无害有妊娠。
弥月不迟,	怀孕十月不延迟,
是生后稷,	生下儿子是后稷。
降之百福,	上天赐予百种福,
黍稷重穋,	黍稷成熟有早晚,
稙⑧穉⑨菽麦。	豆麦先后播下土。

① 憬：觉悟。
② 赂：赠送财物。
③ 閟（bì）：神。閟宫，神庙，指供奉后稷的母亲姜嫄的庙。
④ 侐：清静的样子。
⑤ 实：广大的样子。
⑥ 回：邪。
⑦ 依：凭依。
⑧ 稙：早种的谷物。
⑨ 穉（zhì）：晚种的谷物。

And sing sweet melodies.
The chief of Huai tribes brings
All rare and precious things:
Ivory tusks, tortoise old,
Southern metals and gold.

Hymn to Marquis of Lu[①]

Solemn the temples stand,
Well-built, well-furnished, grand.
There we find Jiang Yuuan's shrine:
Her virtue was divine.
On God she did depend
And safely by the end
Of her ten months was born
Hou Ji, our Lord of Grain or Corn.
Blessed by Heaven, he knew
When sowing time was due
For wheat and millet early or late.

---

① This was the longest epic ode or hymn in praise of Marquis or Duke Xi of Lu, celebrating his magnificent career of success. It was was written by Xi Si on an occasion when the Marquis had repaired on a large scale the temple of the State of Lu.

奄①有下国，	后稷拥有全天下，
俾民稼穑。	教会人民种庄稼。
有稷有黍，	既有高粱和黍子，
有稻有秬②。	还有香稻和黑黍。
奄有下土，	四海之内都归顺，
缵③禹之绪。	大禹事业得承继。
后稷之孙，	说起后稷子孙旺，
实维大④王。	古公亶父谥太王。
居岐之阳，	住在岐山向阳地，
实始翦⑤商。	开始准备灭殷商。
至于文武，	传到文王和武王，
缵大王之绪。	太王事业更发扬。
致天之届，	替天行道伐殷纣，
于牧之野。	牧野一战殷商亡。
"无贰无虞⑥，	"莫怀二心莫欺诳，
上帝临女！"	人人头顶有上苍！"
敦⑦商之旅，	集合殷商之俘获，
克咸厥功。	成就大业世无双。

① 奄：包括。
② 秬：黑黍。
③ 缵：继承。
④ 大(tài)王：文王的祖父古公亶父。
⑤ 翦：消灭。
⑥ 虞：欺骗。
⑦ 敦：聚集。

Invested with a state,
He taught people to sow
The millet and to grow
The sorghum and the rice.
All over the country nice
He followed Yu of xia's advice.

The grandson of Hou Ji
King Tai came to install
Himself south of Mount Qi,
Nearer to Shang capital.
Then came Kings Wen and Wu;
They both followed King Tai.
King Wu beat Shang in Mu,
Decreed by Heaven high.
"You should have nor fear nor doubt
For great God is with you.
You'll wipe Shang forces out,
With victory in view."

王曰叔父①,	成王开口叫叔父,
建尔元子②,	封你长子为侯王,
俾侯于鲁。	使他为王在鲁邦。
大启尔宇③,	大大开拓你土疆,
为周室辅。	辅卫周室做屏障。
乃命鲁公,	成王下令给鲁公,
俾侯于东,	建立侯国在东方。
锡之山川,	赐他山川与土地,
土田附庸④。	还有小国做附庸。
周公之孙,	周公远孙鲁僖公,
庄公之子⑤,	庄公之子是英雄。
龙旂⑥承祀,	打着龙旗来祭祀,
六辔耳耳⑦,	六条缰绳把马控。
春秋匪解,	四时祭祀不懈怠,
享祀不忒。	玉帛牺牲按时供。
皇皇后帝,	光明伟大的上帝,
皇祖后稷,	还有后稷老祖宗。
享以骍牺,	献上牺牲黄色牛,
是飨是宜⑧,	神灵享受兴味浓,
降福既多。	降下洪福千万种。

① 叔父:指周公。
② 元子:长子,指周公的长子伯禽。
③ 宇:居,引申为领土。
④ 附庸:小国。
⑤ 庄公之子:指鲁僖公。
⑥ 龙旂:画着交龙的旗帜。
⑦ 耳耳:华丽的样子。
⑧ 是飨是宜:指两种祭名。

King Cheng said to his uncle great,
"I will set up your eldest son
As Marquis of Lu State
And enlarge the land you have won
To protect the Zhou State."

The Duke of Lu was made
Marquis in the east obeyed,
And given land to cultivate,
Hills, rivers and attached state.
He was Duke of Zhou's grandson
And Duke Zhuang's eldest son.
With dragon banners at command,
He came six reins in hand.
He made his offering
In autumn as in spring
To God in Heaven great
And Hou Ji of Zhou State.
He offered victims nice
For the great sacrifice
And received blessings twice

周公皇祖，	伟大先祖周公旦，
亦其福女。	也将赐你福无穷。
秋而载尝①，	秋天尝祭庆丰收，
夏而楅衡，	夏天设栏先养牛，
白牡骍刚。	公牛有白也有黄。
牺尊②将将，	漂亮酒樽装美酒，
毛炰③胾羹④，	生烤乳猪肉片汤，
笾豆大房⑤。	大盘小碗都装满。
万舞⑥洋洋，	场面盛大百舞跳，
孝孙⑦有庆。	保佑子孙享清福。
俾尔炽而昌，	使你兴旺又昌盛，
俾尔寿而臧。	使你长寿且吉祥。
保彼东方，	愿你能安定东方，
鲁邦是常。	守卫鲁国国运长。
不亏不崩，	江山永固不崩溃，
不震不腾。	如水长流不震荡。
三寿⑧作朋，	寿比三老百年长，
如冈如陵。	稳如丘陵和山岗。

① 尝：秋祭名。
② 牺尊：形状像卧牛的酒杯。
③ 毛炰：去毛的小烤猪。
④ 胾（zì）羹：肉片汤。
⑤ 大房：一种盛大块肉的食器，形如高足盘。
⑥ 万舞：一种舞蹈的名称。
⑦ 孝孙：祭祀的孙子，指僖公。
⑧ 三寿：指上寿、中寿、下寿。

From his ancestors dear;
Even the Duke of Zhou did appear.

In summer came the rite;
In autumn horns were capped of bull.
There were bul'ls red and white,
Bull-figured goblets full,
Roast pig, soup and minced meat,
And dishes of bamboo and wood,
And dancers all-complete.
Blessed be ye grandsons good!
May you live in prosperity
And protect the eastern land!
May you have longevity
And may the land of Lu long stand!
Unwaning moon, unsunken sun,
Nor flood nor earthquake far and nigh.
In long life you are second to none,
And firm as mountain high.

公车千乘，	鲁公兵车有千辆，
朱英绿縢①，	红缨长矛绳缠弓，
二矛重弓。	弓矛一时都具备。
公徒三万，	鲁公步卒有三万，
贝胄②朱绶，	红线缀贝饰盔上，
烝徒增增③。	大军人多势力强。
戎狄是膺④，	痛击北狄和西戎，
荆舒是惩，	荆舒两国受严惩，
则莫我敢承⑤。	谁人还敢反抗我。
俾尔昌而炽，	使你兴旺又繁荣，
俾尔寿而富。	使你长寿又年丰。
黄发台背⑥，	老人驼背头发黄，
寿胥与试。	寿高还把重任扛。
俾尔昌而大，	使你昌盛又强大，
俾尔耆而艾⑦。	使你年高又寿长。
万有千岁，	千年万岁寿无疆，
眉寿⑧无有害。	长命百岁无灾殃。
泰山岩岩⑨，	泰山高峻多险峰，
鲁邦所詹。	鲁国对它最推崇。

① 縢：缠在弓上的丝绳。
② 贝胄：贝壳做的头盔。
③ 增：形容兵士蜂拥前进的样子。
④ 膺：击。
⑤ 承：抵挡。
⑥ 黄发台背：都是老人的象征。
⑦ 耆、艾：都是长寿的意思。
⑧ 眉寿：长寿的特征。
⑨ 岩岩：高峻的样子。

A thousand war chariots were seen;
Each had two spears with tassels red
And two bows bound by bands green.
Thirty thousand men the duke led
In shell-adorned helmets were dressed.
They marched in numbers great
To quell the tribes of north and west
And punish southern state.
None of them could stand your attack.
May you enjoy prosperity!
With hoary hair and wrinkled back,
May you enjoy longevity!
Age will give you advice.
May you live great and prosperous
To a thousand years old or twice!
May you live long and vigorous
As eyebrows long unharmed by vice!

Lofty is Mountain Tai
Looked up to from Lu State.

奄有龟蒙,	龟山蒙山都属鲁,
遂荒大东。	边境一直伸到东。
至于海邦,	还有海滨各属国,
淮夷来同①。	淮夷带头来朝贡。
莫不率从,	无人胆敢不服从,
鲁侯之功。	功劳应归鲁僖公。
保有凫②绎,	保有凫山和绎山,
遂荒徐宅。	徐国也在控制中。
至于海邦,	沿海小国都归附,
淮夷蛮貊③。	淮夷蛮貊都俯首。
及彼南夷,	还有荆楚南夷国,
莫不率从。	没有谁人不服从。
莫敢不诺④,	无人胆敢不听话,
鲁侯是若。	顺从鲁侯态度恭。
天锡公纯嘏⑤,	天赐鲁公大吉祥,
眉寿保鲁。	高寿长命保鲁地。
居常与许⑥,	收回常许两边邑,
复周公之宇。	恢复周公之疆土。
鲁侯燕喜,	鲁侯宴饮多欢喜,
令妻寿母。	贤妻良母受称颂。

① 来同：来朝。
② 凫：凫山，在今山东邹县西南。
③ 蛮貊：东南方的异族。
④ 诺：答应，顺从。
⑤ 纯嘏：大福。
⑥ 常、许，地名。

Mounts Gui and Meng stand nigh
And eastward undulate
As far as eastern sea.
Huai tribes make no ado
But go down on their knee
Before the Marquis Lu.

We have Mounts Fu and Yi
And till at Xu'the ground
Which extends to the sea
Where barbarians are found.
No southern tribe dare disobey
The Marquis of Lu's command;
None but would homage pay
To the Marquis of Lu grand.

Heaven gives Marquis blessings great
And a long life to rule over Lu.
He shall restore Duke of Zhou's State
And dwell at Chang and Xu.
The Marquis feasted his ministers
With his fair wife and mother old

宜大夫庶士，
邦国是有①。
既多受祉，
黄发儿②齿。

徂徕③之松，
新甫④之柏，
是断是度⑤，
是寻是尺。
松桷⑥有舄⑦，
路寝⑧孔硕，
新庙奕奕⑨。
奚斯⑩所作，
孔曼且硕，
万民是若。

大夫诸臣都和睦，
国家始终能兴旺。
既受天赐多福祉，
返老还童长新齿。

徂徕山上长松树，
新甫山上柏树长。
砍下树木又劈开，
用寻用尺细丈量。
松木椽子直又大，
建成宫殿多气派，
新修宗庙真漂亮。
奚斯作成诗一首，
长篇巨制有文采，
人人赞扬好诗才。

① 有：保有。
② 儿（ní）："齯"的假借词。
③ 徂徕：山名，在今山东泰安县东南。
④ 新甫：山名，也叫梁山，在泰山旁。
⑤ 度："剫"的假借词，劈开。
⑥ 桷：方木椽。
⑦ 舄（xì）：粗大的样子。
⑧ 路寝：古代帝王处理政事的宫室。
⑨ 奕奕：同"绎绎"，相连的样子。
⑩ 奚斯：鲁大夫公子鱼。

And other officers
For the state he shall hold.
He shall be blessed with golden hairs
And juvenile teeth like his heir's.

The hillside cypress and pine
Are cut down from the root;
Some as long as eight feet or nine,
Others as short as one foot.
They are used to build temples new
With inner chambers large and long.
Behold! The temples stand in view.
It is Xi Si who makes this song
Which reads so pleasant to the ear
That people witt greet him with cheer.

那

猗①与那与！	多么盛大又富丽！
置我鞉鼓②。	堂上安放拨浪鼓。
奏鼓简简，	鼓儿咚咚响起来，
衎③我烈祖。	用此娱乐我先祖。

汤孙④奏假，	汤孙奏乐告神明，
绥我思成。	赐我太平天下安。
鞉鼓渊渊⑤，	拨浪鼓儿咚咚响，
嘒嘒⑥管声。	箫管呜呜多清亮。
既和且平，	曲调和谐歌太平，
依我磬声。	玉磬配合更悠扬。

於赫汤孙，	商汤子孙真显赫，
穆穆⑦厥声。	他的乐队乐声美。
庸鼓有斁⑧，	敲钟击鼓响铿锵，
万舞有奕。	洋洋万舞好排场。
我有嘉客，	助祭嘉宾已来临，
亦不夷⑨怿！	大家一起喜洋洋！

① 猗（ē）、那：形容乐队盛大的样子。
② 鞉（táo）鼓：一种鼓乐器，类似今天的拨浪鼓。
③ 衎（kàn）：欢乐的意思。
④ 汤孙：商汤的子孙。
⑤ 渊渊：形容鼓声嘈杂。
⑥ 嘒嘒：吹奏管乐器清亮的声音。
⑦ 穆穆：美好的样子。
⑧ 斁：形容乐器声很响亮。
⑨ 夷：喜悦的意思。

Hymn to King Tang[1]

How splendid! How complete!
Let us put drums in place.
Listen to their loud beat,
Ancestor of our race.

Your descendants invite
Your spirit to alight
By resounding drumbeat
And by flute's music sweet.
In harmony with them
Chimes the sonorous gem.

The descendants with cheer
Listen to music bright.
Bells and drums fill the ear
And dancers seem in flight.
Our visitors appear
Also full of delight.

---

[1] This hymn was appropriate to King Tang the successful who overthrew the dynasty of Xia and founded that of Shang in 1765 B.C.. It dwelt on the music and the reverence with which the service was performed.

自古在昔，	遥想古代我先王，
先民有作。	早把祭礼安排好。
温恭朝夕，	态度温和又恭敬，
执事有恪①。	小心谨慎祭祀忙。
顾予烝尝②，	冬祭秋祭神灵来，
汤孙之将。	商汤子孙奉酒浆。

烈　祖

嗟嗟烈祖，	烈烈先祖多荣光，
有秩斯祜③。	不断降下大福祥。
申④锡无疆，	无穷无尽多赐赏，
及尔斯所。	恩泽遍布我国疆。
既载清酤，	先祖神前设清酒，
赉⑤我思成。	赐我国土享安康。
亦有和羹⑥，	还有调和美味汤，
既戒既平。	五味齐全又适当。
鬷⑦假无言，	心中默默向神祷，
时靡有争。	次序井然无争嚷。
绥我眉寿，	神灵赐我百年寿，
黄耇⑧无疆。	满头黄发寿无疆。

① 恪：恭敬的样子。
② 烝尝：冬祭名烝，秋祭名尝。
③ 祜：福气。
④ 申：重、又。
⑤ 赉：赏赐。
⑥ 和羹：调制好的羹汤。
⑦ 鬷（zōng）：同"奏"。
⑧ 眉寿、黄耇（gǒu）：都是长寿的意思。

Our sires since olden days
Showed us the proper ways
To be meek and polite
And mild from morn to night.
May you accept the rite
Your filial grandson pays!

Hymn to Ancestor[1]

Ah! Ah! Ancestor dear,
Shower down blessings here.
Let your blessings descend
On your sons Without end.
Our wine is clear and sweet.
Make our happiness complete.
Our soup is tempered well,
Good in flavor and smell.
We pray but silently:
Bless us with longevity,
White hair and wrinkled brow.
We have no contention now.

---

[1] This was another hymn appropriate to sacrifice to King Tang of Shang, Shang dwelling on the spirits, the soup and the gravity of the service and assisting princes.

约軝错衡，	车毂裹皮辕雕花，
八鸾鸧鸧①。	四马八铃响叮当。
以假以享，	祭告神灵献祭品，
我受命溥将②。	我受天命封土广。
自天降康，	安定幸福从天降，
丰年穰穰③。	五谷丰登多米粮。
来假来飨，	先祖降临受祭飨，
降福无疆。	赐我福分无限量。
顾予烝尝，	冬祭秋祭神赏光，
汤孙之将。	汤孙祭祀情意长。

玄 鸟④

天命玄鸟，	上天命令神燕降，
降而生商⑤，	生育契后才有商，
宅殷土芒芒⑥。	住居殷地多宽广。
古帝命武汤，	当时上帝命成汤，
正⑦域彼四方⑧。	治理天下管四方。
方命厥后，	号令天下众诸侯，
奄有九有。	九州全部为商疆。

---

① 鸧鸧（qiāng qiāng）：铃声。
② 溥将：广大的样子。
③ 穰穰：禾黍众多的样子。
④ 玄鸟：黑色的燕子。玄，黑色，燕子为黑色，故称玄鸟。
⑤ 商：指商朝的始祖契，传说有娀氏之女简狄吞下燕子卵而怀孕，生下契，契建国于商（今河南省商丘）。
⑥ 芒芒：同"茫茫"，广大的样子。
⑦ 正：治理的意思。
⑧ 方：通"旁"，普遍的意思。

In cars with wheels leather-bound,
At eight bells' tinkling sound,
The princes come to pray
We might be blessed for aye.
O give us far and near
Rich harvest year by year!
O ancestor, alight!
May you accept the rite
Your filial grandsons pay
And bless us as we pray!

The Swallow[①]

Heaven sent Swallow down
To give birth to the sire
Of Shang who wore the crown
Of land of Yin entire.
God ordered Martial Tang,
To conquer four frontiers,
To appoint lords of Shang

---

① This hymn was appropriate to a sacrifice in the ancestral temple of Shang. The Sire of Shang was said to be born around 2300 B. C. when his mother bathing in some open place took and swallowed an egg. dropped by a swallow. The Martial Tang founded the dynasty and his grandson moved the capital to Yin. This hymn was intended to do honor to King Wu Ding (1328—1263B. C.).

商之先后①，	商之先王受天命，
受命不殆，	国运长久无祸殃，
在武丁孙子。	武丁子孙有福祥。
武丁孙子，	后裔武丁多贤良，
武王靡不胜②。	成汤事业他承当。
龙旂十乘，	十辆大车插龙旗，
大糦是承。	满载黍稷供享祭。
邦畿③千里，	幅员辽阔上千里，
维民所止，	人民安居好地方，
肇域彼四海。	四海之内都来投。
四海来假，	四方夷狄也来降，
来假祁祁④。	来朝人多纷且忙。
景⑤员维河，	景山四周绕黄河，
殷受命咸宜，	殷受天命最合适，
百禄是何⑥。	享天指福永无疆。

① 先后：先王，指商汤。
② 胜：胜任。
③ 畿：疆域。
④ 祁祁：众多的样子。
⑤ 景：景山，在今河南省商丘县。
⑥ 何：同"荷"，担负，蒙受。

To rule over nine spheres.
The forefathers of Shang
Reigned by Heaven's decree.
King Wu Ding, descendant of Tang.
Now rules overland and sea.
Wu Ding is a martial king,
Victor second to none.
Ten dragon chariots bring
Sacrifice on the run.
His land extends a thousand lis
Where people live and rest.
He reigns as far as the four seas;
Lords come frora east and west.
They gather at the capital
To pay homage in numbers great.
O good Heaven, bless all
The kings of the Yin State!

长 发

浚①哲维商，　　　　　　　深谋明智是商王，
长发②其祥。　　　　　　　上天常常现吉祥。
洪水芒芒，　　　　　　　　远古洪水白茫茫，
禹敷下土方③。　　　　　　大禹治理定四方。
外大国是疆，　　　　　　　扩张夏朝大国界，
幅陨④既长。　　　　　　　幅员由此广且长，
有娀⑤方将，　　　　　　　有娀之国也兴旺，
帝立子生商。　　　　　　　简狄为妃生玄王。

玄王⑥桓拨，　　　　　　　玄王商契真英明，
受小国是达，　　　　　　　受封小国政令行，
受大国是达。　　　　　　　受封大国也能成。
率履⑦不越，　　　　　　　遵守礼法不越轨，
遂视既发。　　　　　　　　遍加视察尽施行。
相土⑧烈烈，　　　　　　　相土治国真威严，
海外有截⑨。　　　　　　　四海诸侯都听命。

① 浚：濬的假借词，明智的意思。
② 长发：常常发现。
③ 方：四方。
④ 幅陨：幅员，疆域。
⑤ 有娀（sōng）：上古国名，在今山西运城。
⑥ 玄王：即契。
⑦ 率履：循礼。
⑧ 相土：契的孙子。
⑨ 有截：即截截，整齐的样子。

The Rise of Shang[①]

The sire of Shang was wise;
Good omens had appeared for long.
Seeing the deluge rise,
He helped Yu stem the current strong,
Extend the state's frontier
And domain far and wide.
He was son born from Swallow queer
And Princess of Rong, its bride.

He held successful sway
Over states large and small.
He followedhis proper way
To inspect all and instruct all,
Xiang Tu, his martial grandson,
Ruled over land and sea he had won.
Heaven's favor divine

---

① This epic ode celebrated Qi the sire of Shang who helped King Yu of the Xia Dynasty to stem the deluge around 2200 B. C.; Xiang Tu his grnadson; Tang the Martial King who founded the Shang Dynasty; and Yi Yin or A Heng, Tang's chief minister, on occasion of a great sacrifice when all the previous kings of the dynasty and the lords of Shang and their famous ministers were honored in the service, probably in the year 1713 B. C.

帝命不违，	上帝之命不敢违，
至于汤齐。	代代相传到成汤。
汤降不迟，	成汤谦卑不怠慢，
圣敬日跻①。	圣明美德日向上。
昭假②迟迟，	虔诚祈祷不停息，
上帝是祗③，	只把上帝来爱敬，
帝命式于九围④。	帝令九州都效仿。
受小球大球，	接受上天大小法，
为下国缀旒⑤。	表率诸侯做榜样。
何⑥天之休，	承蒙老天赐福祥，
不竞不绿⑦，	不竞争来不急躁，
不刚不柔，	不逞强也不示弱，
敷政优优，	施行政令很宽和，
百禄是遒⑧。	百般福禄聚一堂。
受小共大共，	接受小法和大法，
为下国骏厖⑨。	各国诸侯受庇护。
何天之龙⑩，	承蒙上天多宠爱，
敷奏其勇。	施展才能显英勇。

① 跻（jī）：上升的意思。
② 昭假（gé）：虔诚祈祷。
③ 祗（qí）：尊敬的意思。
④ 九围：即九域、九州的意思。
⑤ 缀旒（zhuì liú）：表率、榜样的意思。
⑥ 何：通"荷"，负荷的意思。
⑦ 绿（qiú）：急躁。
⑧ 遒（qiú）：聚会。
⑨ 骏厖（máng）：保佑。
⑩ 龙：通"宠"，荣誉。

Lasted down to the Martial King.
Toward his lords benign,
In praise of God he'd often sing.
His virtue grows day by day;
It is God he reveres.
God orders him to hold sway
And be model to the nine spheres.

He received ensigns large and small
From subordinate princes far and nigh.
He received blessings from gods all
For which he did not seek nor vie.
To lords he was nor hard nor soft;
His royal rule was gentle oft.
He received favors from aloft.

He received tributes large and small
From princes subordinate.
He received favors from gods all;
He showed his valor great.

不震不动，	既不震惊不摇动，
不戁①不竦，	不胆怯也不惶恐，
百禄是总。	百般福禄都聚拢。

武王载旆②，	汤王出征伐夏后，
有虔秉钺。	手拿大斧多刚强。
如火烈烈，	好比烈火熊熊烧，
则莫我敢曷③。	谁敢阻挡缨我锋。
苞有三蘖④，	一根树干三个杈，
莫遂莫达。	没有一株枝叶长。
九有九截，	九州一齐归殷商，
韦顾⑤既伐，	韦顾两国都投降，
昆吾夏桀。	昆吾夏桀也不留。

昔在中叶，	从前商代中期时，
有震⑥且业。	国力强大镇四方。
允也天子，	成汤真是天之子，
降予卿士。	贤卿名士从天降。
实维阿衡⑦，	就是伊尹号阿衡，
实左右商王。	是他辅佐商汤王。

① 戁（nǎn）：恐惧。
② 旆：通"发"，出发。
③ 曷：通"遏"，害。
④ 蘖（niè）：树枝。
⑤ 韦顾：韦、顾都是国名。
⑥ 震：威武的样子。
⑦ 阿衡：伊尹的号。

Unshaken, he was fortified,
Unscared, unterrified.
All blessings came to his side.

His banners flying higher,
His battle-ax in his fist,
The Martial King came like fire
Whom no foe could resist.
Xie Jie was like the roots
Which could no longer grow
When he lost his three shoots,
Wei, Gu, kun Wu, Tang's former foe.
The Martial King destroyed the brutes
And he ruled high and low.

In times when ruled King Tang,
There was prosperity for Shang.
Heaven favored his son
With Premier A Heng to run
The government and state
At left and eight of the prince great.

殷　武

挞^①彼殷武，　　　　　　　殷王大军真迅猛，
奋伐荆楚。　　　　　　　　奋勇挥师伐荆楚。
罙^②入其阻，　　　　　　　长驱直入险阻地，
裒^③荆之旅。　　　　　　　大败楚军捉俘虏。
有截其所^④，　　　　　　　所到之处捷报传，
汤孙之绪。　　　　　　　　商汤子孙赫赫功。

维女荆楚，　　　　　　　　荆楚只帮要听真，
居国南乡。　　　　　　　　一直住在宋南方。
昔有成汤，　　　　　　　　我的远祖是成汤，
自彼氐羌。　　　　　　　　即使僻远如氐羌，
莫敢不来享^⑤，　　　　　　谁人敢不来进贡，
莫敢不来王，　　　　　　　谁人敢不来朝王，
曰商是常^⑥。　　　　　　　都说服从我殷商。

天命多辟^⑦，　　　　　　　上天下令诸侯国，
设都于禹之绩^⑧，　　　　　大禹治水建国邦，
岁事来辟，　　　　　　　　年年祭祀来朝见，
勿予祸适^⑨，　　　　　　　宽大不愿施谴责，

① 挞：迅速的样子。
② 罙："深"的古字。
③ 裒（póu）：俘虏。
④ 有截其所：指楚国土地整齐划一。
⑤ 享：进献。
⑥ 常：服从。
⑦ 辟：诸侯。
⑧ 绩："迹"的假借字。
⑨ 祸：罪过。适，谴责。

Hymn to King Wu Ding[①]

How rapid did Yin troops appear!
They attacked Chu State without fear.
They penetrated into its rear
And brought back many a captive's ear.
Wu Ding Conquered Chu land.
What an achievement grand!

The king gave Chu command,
"South of our state you stand.
In the time of King Tang
Even the tribes of Jiang
Dared not but come to pay
Homage under his sway.
Such was the rule of Shang."

Heaven gave lords its orders
To build their capitals within Yu's borders,
To pay homage each year,
To do their duties, not to fear

---

① This was an epic ode celebrating the war of King Wu Ding against the southern tribe of Chu, its success and the general happiness and virtue of his reign. This hymn was probably made when a special temple was built for him in 1256 B. C.

稼穑匪解。　　　　　　　　切莫松懈误农桑。

天命降监，　　　　　　　　上天在上察四方，
下民有严①。　　　　　　　下民肃敬又端庄。
不僭②不滥，　　　　　　　不敢妄为违礼制，
不敢怠遑③。　　　　　　　不敢怠惰把业荒。
命于下国，　　　　　　　　天子命令我宋国，
封建厥福。　　　　　　　　努力治国福禄多。

商邑翼翼④，　　　　　　　商都繁华又整齐，
四方之极⑤。　　　　　　　它是四方好榜样。
赫赫厥声，　　　　　　　　他有赫赫好名声，
濯濯⑥厥灵。　　　　　　　他的威灵放光芒。
寿考且宁，　　　　　　　　商王长寿又安康，
以保我后生。　　　　　　　保我子孙万代昌。

陟彼景山，　　　　　　　　登上高高景山颠，
松柏丸丸⑦。　　　　　　　苍松翠柏上参天。
是断是迁，　　　　　　　　锯断松柏运回家，
方斫是虔⑧。　　　　　　　斫成柱子削成梁。

① 严：恭敬庄重的样子。
② 僭：越礼。
③ 遑：闲暇。
④ 翼翼：整齐、繁盛的样子。
⑤ 极：榜样、标准。
⑥ 濯濯：光明。
⑦ 丸丸：光滑而笔直的样子。
⑧ 斫：砍。虔，截断。

Its punishment severe
If farmwork is well done far and near.

Heaven ordered the lords to know
The reverent people below.
They should do no wrong nor be
Indolent and carefree,
To each subordinate state
May be brought blessings great!

The capital was full of order,
A model for states on the border.
The king had great renown
And brilliance up and down.
He enjoyed longevity.
May he bless his posterity!

We climbed the mountain high
Where pine and cypress pieiced the sky.
We felled them to the ground
And hewed them square and round.

松桷^①有梴^②,　　　　　松树椽子长又长,
旅楹有闲,　　　　　　　根根柱子多粗壮,
寝成孔安。　　　　　　　寝庙建成神灵安。

① 桷(jué):方的椽子。
② 梴(chān):木材长长的样子。

We built with beams of pine
And pillars large and fine
The temple for Wu Ding's shrine.

图书在版编目（CIP）数据

许渊冲译诗经：汉文、英文 / 许渊冲译. -- 北京：中译出版社，2021.7

（许渊冲英译作品）

ISBN 978-7-5001-6443-2

Ⅰ. ①许… Ⅱ. ①许… Ⅲ. ①古体诗－诗集－中国－春秋时代－汉、英 Ⅳ. ①I222.2

中国版本图书馆CIP数据核字(2020)第242935号

出版发行	中译出版社
地　　址	北京市西城区车公庄大街甲4号物华大厦6层
电　　话	(010)68359719
邮　　编	100044
电子邮箱	book@ctph.com.cn
网　　址	http://www.ctph.com.cn
出 版 人	乔卫兵
总 策 划	刘永淳
责任编辑	刘香玲　张　旭
文字编辑	王秋璎　张莞嘉　赵浠彤
营销编辑	毕竞方　顾　问
中文注释	周晓宇
封面制作	刘　哲
内文制作	黄　浩　冯　兴
印　　刷	山东临沂新华印刷物流集团有限责任公司
经　　销	新华书店
规　　格	840mm×1092mm　1/32
印　　张	30.125
字　　数	1000千
版　　次	2021年7月第1版
印　　次	2021年7月第1次

ISBN 978-7-5001-6443-2　定价：108.00元

版权所有　侵权必究

中译出版社